# THE MAGIC WAND

Clydean O'Conner

Jacket Design by Mary Helen Preston

Library of Congress - United States Copyright Office

Copyright © by Clydean O'Conner

All rights reserved. ISBN: 9780981945538

# DEDICATION

This fable is dedicated to all the men and women who contributed to my forty-year adventure in a city which should not have survived its desert conditions. Las Vegas pleasure palaces were filled with casino bosses with the souls of black-hearted pirates, and women climbing a slippery corporate ladder coated with the slime of prejudice and sexual harassment.

The Las Vegas casino industry was also populated with people whose hearts were pure gold and should have been cherished employees. But a casino is a soulless place filled with women turned old and bitter before their time and men whose lives are dedicated to the pursuit of money.

# ACKNOWLEDGEMENTS

This book would not have been possible without the help of friends and family members who came to my aid when I needed it most: Rachel Korfman, David Sadleir, Mark and Sue Potes, Cheryl O'Gara and Jeffery Bissel, and a Rottweiler named Anubis who sat by my side and assured there was life after the casino industry.

# CHAPTER ONE
## *Gwen Goes To Vegas*

A few weeks before the year 2022, a fairy godmother from Golfinsphere entered the lives of six people living in Las Vegas--four girls and two guys. Because people living at the dawn of the age of technology thought fairy godmothers only existed in fables, they were under the impression she was just another ordinary person beside whom they worked every day. Like all fairy godmothers, she possessed a magic wand and a hand-held, smaller than a modern-day cellular flip-phone, digital screen through which she could see into the heart of everyone within a seventy-five-mile radius. In sophisticated terminology, this incredible device was called a PPM--short for People Peering Modem.

The fairy godmother, a lady named Gwen, which is *very short* for Gwendolyn, was recently offered a position on planet earth. Extremely smart, Gwen prepared for her mission by reading lots of books written about human beings to better understand them while finishing up her bachelor's degree in Fairyship at the University of the Universal, where she graduated at the top of her class.

After a tedious graduation ceremony, the Supreme Wizard of Golfinsphere personally outlined the responsibilities of her new assignment. She was to seek out the wretched, find the miserable, locate the lonely and identify clinically depressed people using a prescription bottle to cure their woes. Once she isolated appropriate candidates, Gwen was to convince them they could enjoy a better way of life by changing their attitude about the condition in which they found themselves. Unfortunately, it was not unusual for a fairy godmother to spend years perfecting her craft. Even though it was a struggle to work with human beings, every fairy godmother worth her magic wand wanted to move up the corporate ladder to the next rung--Guardian Angel!

Searching for the perfect location in which to fulfill her contract with the Supreme Wizard, Gwen was attracted to a unique landscape on a shiny blue planet by a bright light coming from the top of a pyramid; which she discovered was next door to a castle; that was across the street from a tropical island; and diagonal from the biggest emerald green building Gwen had ever laid eyes on! Despite miles of brilliant LED, all of which seemed to be blinking with enough speed to bring on a seizure, the city appealed to Gwen because most of the people in the enchanted kingdom didn't seem happy.

Using her educational background and credentials earned in Golfinsphere, which the woman in the human resources department thought was someplace in Idaho, Gwen landed a job at a big 'Strip' casino--through whose doors thousands of customers passed every day. Via the incredible software of the PPM--a parting gift from the Supreme Wizard--she could peer into the private lives of both employees and customers in any casino. Oh, she wasn't trying to be snoopy, but she needed to find out what barriers held them back from leading a full and *happy* life. Gwen soon learned casinos were virtual cesspools of human misery.

At first things went badly. Gwen's superiors were put off by the fact she could process the work of three ordinary people. Back in Golfinsphere, everyone *always* worked to their full potential. Golfinspherans were taught never to stop until the job was done. Her excellence in this area earned Gwen a full-ride scholarship to Universal "U". While this quality was much admired in Golfinsphere, on earth the practice made others nervous-- especially insecure department managers. It seemed to Gwen most people thought of work as a place to *go*--not something to *do* with gusto, enthusiasm, and most of all enjoyment.

She was soon transferred from the front desk to room reservations and from there to the food and beverage department because no one seemed to trust her upbeat, pleasant attitude. Co-workers couldn't believe she *enjoyed* coming to work! Despairing of ever understanding the human condition, Gwen put in a call to the Supreme Wizard on the emergency help line, 14-4-40. When he finally called back (he'd been very busy with an extreme situation on another planet involving a political uprising which threatened to obliterate the entire Wambamere nation), the Wizard explained to Gwen she was on her own.

"Once you accept the coveted position of fairy godmother and all its wonderful benefits, it's up to you to find ingenious methods of helping humans out of their muddle," the Supreme Wizard said in a kindly voice.

"Benefits," Gwen snorted, "what benefits? Drudgery, it's all drudgery down here. I slave away, day after day, and get nothing for my trouble! I'm sick and tired of this awful place. I want to come home--now!"

"My, my," the Supreme Wizard said, with a hint of amusement in his voice, "you *are sounding* more and more like a human being! As to the benefits of being a fairy godmother--why, Gwen the list goes on forever. Let's see--where to begin?" The Supreme Wizard laid a finger aside his nose, a twinkle lit his eyes, and his cheeks were rosy. It was maddening because he looked positively cheery! "Well, for one thing, you never grow old. You never need to worry about sagging skin, flabby arms, or a drooping fanny!

Think about all the money you'll save by never needing a face lift and all the hours you can spend doing something you enjoy instead of sweating on an exercise bicycle in a smelly old gym. You'll never have to worry about how awful the casino's health care benefits are because you never get sick! And, fairy godmothers are completely self-supporting, so you don't have to put up with a miserable boss--you're only working in a casino to help other people and there's no shortage of employees who need you in such a wretched place. Their relationships are easy to decode because you've got a magic wand to tell you what's wrong. Besides, once you make Guardian Angel, the most tiresome thing you'll have to do is report in at my weekly staff meeting!"

"Well," Gwen was more than a little sheepish, "I guess I don't have it so bad after all."

"That's a girl! Now get back into the game. Go win one for the Gipper!"

More than a little depressed, Gwen wondered what a Gipper was and what she should win for such a creature. When the screen on the PPM went dark, Gwen felt a surge of panic. Sure, she'd signed a contract with the Wizard, and initially she'd been excited about the human salvage project--but--but, well, maybe things would work better if she could find a Gipper and get it to help her!

Determined to make things better in the casino, Gwen made an appointment with the vice president in charge of human resources. "Mr. Edwards, I'd like to volunteer to write a column for the property newsletter."

Mr. Edwards peered down a nose a bit too long for the rest of his face. "Why would you want to do that?"

"Well," Gwen was beginning to feel defensive, "I'd like to inspire people who work here to live up to their full potential."

"And you don't think employees at our casino are doing that right now?"

"Oh, no, Mr. Edwards. Most of the people I know don't even like their jobs," Gwen said in all sincerity.

The vice president of human resources went pale. He was extremely proud of programs he'd put in place to benefit his workers--like decorating the employee dining room for holidays with crepe paper and cardboard symbols representing different holidays. Why, the EDR (an acronym for employee dining room) was bright and cheery now. And what about the healthy living salad bar--and the food was free. Who did this impertinent young woman think she was? Why, he'd even arranged for punch and cookies to be served at the blood drive! He was sure if he thought a moment longer, he'd be able to come up with a whole list of other benefits he instituted to satisfy the ungrateful horde of dealers and maids--some of whom didn't even speak English! These important benefits were what made working at the Swami Hotel and Casino so terrific. "And just what makes you think you're qualified for such a task? After all," the Vice President of Human Resources glared down the length of his nose at Gwen, "you're *just* a cashier in the coffee shop!"

"I know . . . but I've read a lot of books," Gwen offered.

"Miss, uh, Miss . . . " he glanced at the file on his desk, "Miss Angel, my what an odd name, why don't you go back to your workstation and make sure your weekly drawer report is finished on time. *That's* what you're getting paid to do!"

Disheartened, Gwen realized after her conversation with the exasperated vice president most people were unhappy with their jobs because they were boxed in on all sides by job descriptions written by *corporate* Vice Presidents of Human Resources, who needed the word "human" taken out of their title because they'd lost touch with people a long time ago!

Back at her register, shuffling comp slips and receipts from one pile to another, Gwen looked around at other employees in her department. Most were young, because the wage scale was too low for experienced adults responsible for children, car payments, mortgages, utilities, and food--but there *was* a sprinkling of gray hair here and there. As she studied heads lowered over next week's schedule and the glassy eyes of the day shift bar manager affixed to his hypnotic computer screen, Gwen realized all sense of hope was leached from their faces. Frustration with corporate procedures and boredom with an endless series of unfulfilling tasks was the common denominator in every expression.

Just then, the PPM began to glow. The Supreme Wizard wanted to talk to her! A rush of excitement came over Gwen. Maybe if she let one of the more unfortunate employees in the coffee shop know she had direct contact with the Supreme Wizard, who with a single word of advice could change the course of human events once and for all, perhaps she'd be able to accomplish her mission. The glow was growing intense--the Wizard wanted to speak to her immediately!

"Who should I bring in contact with the Wizard? Who needs his help the most?" she wondered, half to herself and half to the likeness emblazoned on the small digital screen.

Her gaze landed on Betty Anderson. She was a big woman with red hair far too bright to be a product of genetics. In her middle '50s and overweight by forty pounds, Betty acted like she'd spent her life eating sour apples. Using her weight and age as a shield, Betty made sure *all* her gloomy expectations were met. Confident, Gwen asked Betty to step into the food prep area which was vacant now that the lunch rush was over. Withdrawing the hand-held device from her pocket, she expected Betty to be filled with awe at the sight of the Wizard's wondrous face. Instead, Gwen got hostility.

"I don't want one. I can't afford it anyway. My car needs brakes and the taxes on my condo just went up. And this place--well, the three percent raise I got for busting my rear out there--it's not even going to cover the rate hike the electric company pushed through the state legislature. Then there's gas prices which are sky high courtesy of the President of these United States! I've got no money for toys. I'll bet the silly thing isn't even programmed for video poker! What am I going to do with it anyway? Watch the soaps at my station? Sure, just my luck the VP of F&B and that suck-up Director of his would see me standing in one spot, instead of running around like a chicken with my head cut off wiping down tables I cleaned a few minutes ago. My life *is* a soap opera. I gotta kid on drugs and a daughter that's hanging out with a biker. I expect her to turn up pregnant any day now. All they do is hang around the house! They want me to feed them, clean up after them--everything!"

"Really, Betty, this could change your life!" Gwen sputtered.

"Are you into some kinda pyramid scheme? You want me to sell these to all my relatives, friends, and neighbors? My relatives are bums. I got no friends, and I don't even know my neighbors. I'm not about to go knockin' on doors like I was a gadget selling Avon lady!" Betty stomped off, indignant with Gwen for imposing on her valuable time.

"But, but!" Gwen called after Betty as she lumbered out of the kitchen, stopping all her co-workers to warn them Gwen was involved in a weird scam and would be asking them for money soon.

The Wizard was gloating when Gwen glanced back at the PPM screen. "Harder than you thought, huh? *Now you know how I feel!*"

Gwen was speechless. She'd been *so sure* all she had to do was show Betty the cosmic communication device. The Wizard was all powerful--all knowing! What was wrong with Betty anyway? Then a thought occurred to Gwen, and she queried the Wizard. "Say, since you know everything, why didn't you send me here with a set of instructions for solving the problems of these dreadful people? I need a manual for dealing with inferiority, anxiety and guilt!"

The Wizard chuckled. "That's for you to figure out, my dear. It's one way of determining whether you'd make a good Guardian Angel. They must be resourceful; you know--what with the mess a human can make of *everything*. If I gave you all the answers then this wouldn't be much of a test, would it, Gwen?"

Gwen felt like crying. Maybe she wasn't cut out to occupy a rung on the cosmic corporate ladder after all. Maybe she wasn't smart enough, brave enough, or emotionally strong enough to assume such a big responsibility. She wanted to go back to her sprite position. All a sprite had to do was report on conditions--they *never* had to solve any problems!

"Tut, tut, my dear," the Supreme Wizard counseled, "stop second guessing yourself *and* the Supreme Wizard! I have faith in you, even if you don't have much in yourself right now. Chin up, old girl! If I didn't think you could do it, I wouldn't have given you the job. Remember, problems are just opportunities in disguise."

The screen went blank, and Gwen had to quell the urge to dial 14-4-40 and get the Wizard back to give him a piece of her mind. Opportunity? @!! Disguise?? @@**!! Nothing was going right down here. Nobody wanted to listen to advice that could solve all their petty human problems. And, and--how dare the Supreme Wizard cut her off like that!

It was time for a break, so she hurried down to the basement. Before she turned into the employee dining room, Gwen thought she'd better head for the restroom because she felt like bursting into tears. No one would see her cry if she could make it to a bathroom stall in time. Although it took a few moments to gather her composure, Gwen decided she was not going to end her career sitting on a toilet, wiping her nose, in a grungy employee bathroom in the basement. So, she stood up, wiped her nose again, and rushed out of the stall door. Gwen glanced in the mirror over the sink, where all female employees routinely checked their make-up because HR posted a sign warning them to look their best before returning to the casino. Her face was red, her eyes puffy, her fists were clenched, and she was breathing hard and fast. Why--why--she looked positively human! "Oh my, I guess I've been on earth too long." Gwen shoved the PPM back into her pocket. She shrugged her shoulders, trying her best to put the experience with Betty behind her.

When she returned to the corner in the kitchen where she worked on a make-shift desk, Gwen began to review the vacation schedules for the entire department. Trying to make sure every job was covered by someone, who was cross trained to fill another position, and wasn't planning to go on vacation at the same time, gave her a headache.

Gwen was discouraged by the impossible mess human beings made of their lives when all they had to do was following Supreme Wizard's three basic tenants:

1. *Don't hurt anyone deliberately.* In her time on earth, Gwen learned people did enough damage to others by accident and premeditated harm was like a boomerang it came right back because thoughts were just as real as bullets and twice as deadly!

2. *Keep on striving.* Gwen already knew how important it was for people to set a few goals and then never, ever stop reaching for them. Of equal importance was to keep goals expandable because life is about attaining. Oh, not just goods and services, but the strengthening and expansion of a person's mental, emotional, and philosophical horizons. It was important for everyone to have another hill to climb because Gwen observed boredom killed far more people than disease! Even if one person's goals made no sense to anyone else--like the man living in the middle of the Sahara Desert who was determined to climb Mt. Everest before the age of fifty. Or the woman who couldn't carry a tune in a bucket but practiced every day in hopes of becoming an opera star, so she could sing a duet with a world-famous tenor. Everyone needed to learn to have faith in themselves!

3. *Be kind.* This seemed to be the most important of the Supreme Wizard's rules because Gwen felt there was an extreme lack of kindness on earth. Instead of shouting at the kids, the wife, neighbors, and the stupid idiot in the red car on the freeway, Gwen knew kindness smoothed the bumps in life's road. Like a stone thrown in a pond, kindness eddied in ever widening circles. For instance, Gwen complimented a VIP Services girl on her new hairdo this morning. The girl was so pleased she was

extra nice to the next customer, who gave the bellman a big tip because he was friendly and offered an excellent suggestion about a local restaurant which served his favorite kind of food. The bellman left the cook five dollars in a tip cup in the EDR because the eggs were cooked just the way the bellman liked them! Acts of kindness were always rewarded--even if the effect wasn't immediately obvious.

It was so strange on earth, not all like Golfinsphere. For the most part, people were not nice. They said things to hurt each other and went out of their way to sabotage both friends and family, especially when it came to the dating scene. Jealousy was rampant and competition for the beautiful girl or the handsome jock was fierce. It was all so weird, and Gwen was homesick for all the rational people in her world. No one ever got their feelings hurt--in fact, now that she thought about it--she wondered if anyone in Golfinsphere at feelings at all? No one was ever upset, angry, frustrated, disgusted, intimidated, shy, disappointed--why hadn't she noticed this before? Negative emotions were all she seemed to run into on earth. Gwen went to bed depressed and for the first time in her life she wondered what she'd gotten into.

# CHAPTER TWO
## *The Trouble With Trish*

How and where to start on Trish? My, oh my--it was a big problem. Although this was her first experience in changing the conditions of a human's life, on her list of candidates Gwen thought Trish's inferiority complex might be the easiest to remedy.

Gwen watched Trish pause in front of every mirror she passed. Other women in the office spoke behind their hands and whispered about Trish over lunch. Some of the older office crones could be as cruel as any of the outcast witches in Golfinsphere.

"There she goes again," cackled Jane.

"She acts like a peacock--all that strutting and preening," chimed in June.

"Blot your lipstick dear . . . no one's going to kiss you anyway." Teresa yowled like a stretching cat.

"Will you look at her fluff her hair? Where does she think she's going--to a ball? And she's nearly thirty, you'd think she'd be smart enough to give up looking for Prince Charming by now," Penny clucked as she plucked the lint from her sweater.

Trish knew the other women were gossiping about her. She also knew how to annoy them, so she sashayed over to the new Director of VIP Services, who was a dead ringer for Brad Pitt.

"Hi, Jay," she said in her most charming tone of voice.

"Uh--Uh . . ." Fresh out of college, Jay was flustered by receiving attention from a woman he considered beautiful, sophisticated, and out of his league.

Trish glanced back at the hens clustered around the coffee pot, who, as far as she was concerned, might as well have been scratching the ground for seeds. All eyes were trained on her. Winding her finger in his tie, Trish drew the red-faced young man closer to her red, pouting lips. "How about a drink after work one night this week?"

June wanted to peck Trish's eyes out. She'd been trying to get up the nerve to ask Jay for drinks herself.

"Uh . . . I'd love to!" Good fortune was coming to Jay in buckets. Landing a job at the Swami Hotel and Casino, the only five-start resort on The Strip, was a feather in his cap and, now--this!

"Who does she think she is?" Jane's feathers were ruffled because Trish always got everything and everyone she wanted.

"She'd do *anything* to get a man," Penelope squawked, her voice so high and piercing it carried across the space filled with cubicles.

Trish smiled and strolled back to her desk, hips swaying. She fluffed her hair again, preening into the mirror above her computer. The office hens were captured in the reflection, scratching and pecking and gesturing in Trish's direction. She knew a date with Jay would be the topic of office gossip for a long, long time.

Later that day, Gwen noticed the dismay in Trish's eyes as she stood at the copier working on a big presentation. She would press her hands against her abdomen, as though willing her stomach to flatten. Then she'd pound on her hips with her fists--whether in frustration or in hope of tenderizing the muscle for a thinner profile, Gwen couldn't tell. Just then, Betty Anderson waddled into the Xerox room. "You're nothing but skin and bones, deary! If you ask me, you look like a scarecrow. Look at your arm--it's a stick. There's not a man alive who wants to cuddle up to a bag of bones!"

Trish bristled and pushed the collator button so hard the machine jammed. Trish tried to brush Betty off, but she was hurt by the older woman's remark.

"When was the last time you had a date, deary? Maybe that's why you're so glum all the time. None of us can say a word to you without getting our heads snapped off. The other girls try to stay out of your way but I'm sick and tired of your snotty attitude. You're never gonna get a man acting like you're some kinda prime real estate, honey. You're no better than the rest of us so get down off your high horse and stop acting like you are royalty--*you ain't no Duchess*."

Betty was pleased. The whole office had been egging her on to put Trish in her place. And she was so proud of herself she didn't notice the tears in Trish's eyes or the crushed expression on her face as the younger woman rushed from the room.

In her bathroom late that night, Trish examined her face for signs of age and slathered on expensive goo, which promised to reverse the eroding onslaught of nature.

"That girl is stunning--why does she think she looks lumpy and frumpy?  I wonder how in heaven's name she got such a poor image of herself."  Gwen pondered the situation and adjusted the PPM dial to go back in time--to Trish's childhood--in an effort to discover the reason for the distorted way she saw herself.  The screen was as fuzzy as a Montana road in a blizzard when Gwen twisted the knobs on the cosmic communication device trying to locate the frequency which would connect her to the unhappy girl's past.  Finally, the screen cleared and an image of a three-year old girl sitting at a kitchen table appeared.

Agitated, her mother was brushing the child's fine, silky hair.  "Hold still!  I can't do anything with your hair.  We're late for church.  This mop is so unruly it reminds me of your father's hair.  It flies everywhere.  It's so hard to make you presentable!  All I can do now is wet your hair down and make braids.  I hate to do that because your ears stick out, but oh well, it's all I have time for now.  I can just hear Mrs. Johnson.  She'll whisper behind her fan that she's never seen such ears big ears on a little girl.  I hope she doesn't start calling you 'Dumbo' in Sunday school!"

No wonder Trish spent hours with a curling iron and sprayed her hair so stiff it wouldn't move in a hurricane velocity wind!  Gwen adjusted the dial forward a few years and tuned in on Trish's childhood again.

Sadly, she found the same situation--just a different topic.  Trish was dressed for the church social, and her mother was criticizing her choice of clothing.  "For heaven sake, Patricia, the sleeves of that blouse are too short.  You're growing again!  I hope you don't become a giant.  You could, you know, your father is tall.  It would be awful if you take after him.  You're already the talk of the entire congregation.  Why, everyone says you'll be six feet before you stop growing.  What will happen to you then?  You'll probably never get married because no boy wants a girl towering over him!"

Gwen had to admit Trish was tall for fourteen, but what the poor girl didn't realize was by the time she graduated from high school all the boys would shoot past her and she would be a full head shorter than many of the other girls in her class.

"She doesn't know she's *not* huge *or* gangly," Gwen fussed.  "Trish never realized she's just average for a human being. And at a hundred and twenty pounds, why, Trish is on the thin side according to the medical chart I saw the other day!"

Gels and hair spray gave her hair body and substance now, but Trish's view of herself had been formed at an early age. Unfortunately, that image clung to her like a bad haircut!

Compliments didn't change her self-concept either. Trish ignored flattering remarks because she didn't believe them, so Gwen moved the PPM ahead two more years.

"You drive me crazy!" Trish's mother shouted. "Look at you-- you're the picture of your father, and that's not a pretty sight!"

Trish was heartbroken. She'd honestly thought her mother would be pleased at the condition of the garage. The entire day was spent sorting through boxes and piles of junk. True, her hands were dirty, her clothes grimed and her hair a mess--but the garage was now so spacious her mother could park the car inside.

"Well," Gwen was fuming, "how was Trish supposed to know one of her mother's biggest complaints about her father was how much time he spent messing with things that got his hands dirty?" A tinkerer, her Dad spent hours in the shed out back--both to indulge in his passion for mechanical devices *and* to escape his wife's constant harping. "Trish wasn't old enough to understand her parents suffered the slings and arrows of a lousy relationship!" Gwen was disgusted with Trish's mother and infuriated her father never came to the child's defense.

What to do? Gwen tapped the magic wand against her forehead. While contemplating the problem, a small amount of fairy dust fell on the desk. It sparkled in the sun and particles of crystalline dust refracted a dozen scintillant rainbows throughout the room. While watching motes of fairy dust dance through the air, a thought came to Gwen. That was it! She was so excited about the solution to Trish's problem Gwen nearly fell off the worn leather chair she purchased at a second-hand store downtown.

That weekend, Gwen haunted every dumpy store in downtown Las Vegas looking for the right item. Hot, tired, and growing desperate, Gwen was in a foul mood, which was *very* unbecoming to a fairy godmother because they started to resemble the trolls who lived under a major thoroughfare in Golfinsphere. Attracted by the charm of an orchid-colored building with white shutters framing each window, Gwen decided this was going to be her last stop. If she didn't find what she was looking for there--she'd have to rethink the solution to Trish's problem.

She poked into dresser drawers, dug through cardboard boxes, and sorted through a bunch of old picture frames. Just as she was about to give up on her quest, the owner of the shop came through the door with a gunny sack filled with things he'd picked up at an estate sale in Sacramento. There, consigned to the bottom of the burlap bag, lay the very item Gwen was seeking . . . an antique mirror. Although black with tarnish, the silver frame held promise. Gwen paid far too much for the mirror, but she was still having trouble with the concept of money. Back in Golfinsphere, "rich" was a state of mind and had nothing at all to do with the balance in a checkbook. Oh, if someone was interested in accumulating worthless doodads, knick-knacks and other folderol, it was perfectly okay--but contentment and happiness provided the rock-solid foundation of a portfolio on Golfinsphere.

After cleaning away years of tarnish, Gwen applied a liberal application of fairy dust. Then she rattled off a complicated series of instructions to bring about enchantment. Now--the mirror would only reflect Trish's best physical attributes!

A few days later, on Trish's birthday, Gwen presented the gift. Trish was enthralled by the mirror's beautiful design, but she had no idea it was a magic mirror. The next morning, as Trish began the rituals by which she got ready for work, she glanced in the magic mirror.

"Funny," she thought, "my skin really looks different today." Examining the lights surrounding the mirror above the bathroom vanity, Trish satisfied herself all the bulbs were burning brightly. Then she looked outside to see whether the sun was shining. Just like any other day in Las Vegas, the sun was brilliant, and the sky was clear. "Maybe it's that new anti-aging cream I bought last week," Trish said as she studied her face. "It really seems to be working!"

Applying a final squirt of hairspray with a flourish, Trish reached for the magic mirror to check the back of her hair. "My," she thought with surprise which gave way to delight, "this brand of gel certainly holds the curl. My hair looks as good as Prince William's future queen!"

Arriving at work in a better mood than she had in days, Trish shocked everyone in the office by saying, "Good morning!"

"Find a man last night, Trish?" Betty Anderson said, her voice oozing venom. She couldn't tolerate Trish's bright smile and did her best to provoke the normally volatile young woman.

"Not yet! Maybe later this week--if I'm lucky," Trish said breezily in response to Betty's nasty remark.  Then, to the surprise of the whole office, Trish went to work on the stack of correspondence in the middle of her desk. There was no stomping, no slamming drawers, no exasperated sighs which declared the nerdy little casino analyst on the night shift left most *his* work for *her* to complete--again!

After lunch, Trish pulled the antique mirror from her purse to fix her lipstick.  When she ran her tongue over her teeth to remove any traces of wilted lettuce served in the EDR, Trish stared into the mirror.  She smiled, then shifted in her seat to catch the afternoon light streaming through the only window in the office.  "Funny, my teeth seem whiter today than they did yesterday."  Trish was perplexed.  She hadn't changed brands of toothpaste-- yet her teeth looked as if she'd been using the expensive whitening treatment hawked on an infomercial hosted by a movie star she admired.  "Weird," she thought as she put the mirror back in her purse and returned to work with gusto.

Her fingers flew over the computer keyboard and when her boss got back from an extended lunch, he was dumbfounded by the number of completed reports and the stack of correspondence.  Although he scrutinized every piece of paper, Trish's work was flawless--and--and, she was humming instead of fuming!  Nervously, he adjusted his tie, bracing for the scathing remark which must be on the horizon like a looming storm cloud.  Trish was the best assistant he'd ever found, and it made him endure her viperous tongue and acid retorts, which were always directed at his emotional Achilles heel.  It was a good thing casino tradition kept women in low-level management jobs or he might have to worry about his position.  As it was, he felt comfortable using Trish to make himself look good because raises, titles and perks were the exclusive domain of the good old boys' club!

Before she went to bed, Trish smeared the expensive lotion on her face with a generous hand.  Maybe it *was* worth the price she'd paid for it. Maybe *this* jar was going to live up to the saleswoman's promises.  When she awoke the next morning and examined her eyes--they seemed almost as beautiful as Elizabeth Taylor's, except she had no sign of crow's feet.  Her face was positively glowing, and Trish sang along with the radio while she took a shower.

As she checked to make certain the zipper was closed all the way up the back of her dress, Trish noticed her hips looked a little smaller.  "Finally," she whooped, "this new diet is starting to work!  I'll look as good as Jennifer Aniston before long!"  Trish skipped to her car and raced down the freeway without yelling at a single driver to get out of her way.  "Boy, the traffic was sure light today," she thought to herself as she locked her car.

14

"Hi, Trish," the employee lot security guard said tentatively, expecting Trish to give him a dirty look for having the nerve to speak to her.

"Hey, how's it going, Jim?" Trish's tone was breezy.

Encouraged by her smile, the guard decided to offer a compliment although he was usually rebuffed. "You sure look nice today. Is that dress new?"

Trish glanced at the bright red dress she'd worn at least a hundred times. "No, it's not, but thanks anyway. Have a good day--don't melt in all this heat!"

If the pavement hadn't been so hot, Jim would have fallen over backward. This was the first pleasant thing the pretty girl ever said to him. Maybe today's conversation was just an accident, but he made up his mind to speak to Trish again tomorrow.

Trish greeted bellmen, front desk clerks, casino porters, dealers and even a pit boss she disliked with a cheery smile and a friendly hello. Astonished expressions followed in her wake.

Gwen was so happy with the change in Trish's attitude she wanted to call the Supreme Wizard to report her project was working out even better than she expected, but the line was busy when she dialed 14-4-40. When *was* the Supreme Wizard going to install call waiting?

The magic mirror was having such a positive effect on Trish's personality, even the General Manager took note. Before many more weeks passed, Trish was offered a management position in the catering department, which left the casino analyst high and dry. His extended lunches stopped, and he had to work late to finish the reports Trish normally whipped out so fast.

When the iPONG convention came to town, Trish made all kinds of reservations and provided other exceptional services to every exhibitor and delegate. It was under those circumstances she met James. He was surprised at how quickly she mastered the intricacies of the iPONG industry.

"Why don't you make Halloween iPONGs? Parents would be happy to give them out instead of candy. Kids already love them, and parents won't have to worry about some weirdo poisoning apples," Trish offered after examining one of the little circles encoded with circuitry which made them morph from one image to another.

"Say, that's an excellent idea, Trish." James found himself smiling from ear to ear. "I'm going to call my production manager right now. If we get them into production right away, we can just make Halloween."

"How about getting retailers to use them as part of their advertising? If kids know they can get five free iPONGs when their parents buy a gallon of frozen butterscotch custard--they'll whine for it until the one of the parents give in!" Trish glanced up from the iPONG in her hand and realized James had the most captivating smile she'd ever seen.

"Say, where did you get your marketing degree?" he asked.

"I don't have a degree but ideas just seem to pop into my head all the time." Trish's natural reserve began to thaw beneath the warmth of James' attention.

"And excellent ideas they are!" James was sincere--he felt as though he'd stumbled across buried treasure.

"You really think so?" Trish asked, her radar extended to detect a come-on.

"I certainly do! And just to prove what I think about your idea, I'm going to authorize the controller at iPONG to send you a check for $10,000 . . . and that's just an advance on your idea. I'm going to give you one percent of everything we net on Halloween iPONGs." James pushed four on his cell phone and started talking to the controller.

"Wow" Trish thought to herself. "Whenever I brought an idea to the attention of the casino manager, he just patted me on the head and told me to go away."

When he finished with the controller James asked to be transferred to the production manager at the iPONG plant; and then told the operator to get the VP over the sales department on the line. Looking somewhat sheepish, he returned his attention to Trish. "The Halloween iPONGs will be off the line in two weeks and the sales department thinks they are going to fly off the shelves. I think I need to cancel that check!" James said.

Trish was crestfallen. Just when she thought she'd come up with a promising idea . . . James wasn't serious, just like all the creeps in the casino she'd been working with for years.

"The vice president of sales thinks my sales projection is too small. I'm afraid $10,000 isn't a big enough advance--we're going to pay you $15,000 for your idea."

Before long, James asked Trish to join his iPONG manufacturing

16

company as Vice President of New Trend Development. Not long afterward, Gwen thought she was going to explode when James took Trish's hand on the star-studded night he proposed marriage to the sound of cellos playing on the satellite radio station in his Ferrari.

On her wedding day, Trish checked her make-up in the magic mirror one last time before she headed down the aisle. Everything was flawless--the elegant lace gown, the flowers in her hair, the sparkle in her eyes. As Gwen straightened the train of Trish's wedding dress, she basked in the glow of a beautiful young woman about whom the only thing that really changed was her perception of herself.

When the doors to the chapel opened, Trish took her father's arm. She looked back, just once, to wink at Gwen as the wedding march began to play. Then she floated down the aisle toward her new life with Prince Charming, who was destined to become the iPONG king of America.

# CHAPTER THREE
## *Brenda Takes The Blame*

Brenda was almost fifty-five, and while that was considered middle-age, it hardly meant life was over in the twentieth century. Gwen liked Brenda--a lot. She was sweet, sensitive and was always there for her friends. What Gwen couldn't understand was why such a nice lady was always apologizing. Apologizing if the computer went down; apologizing if the waiter didn't bring the correct lunch order; apologizing to the casino manager if the weekend report was late--even when the computer system froze because the corporate IT department tried to upgrade a software platform, or some other unforeseen situation, over which Brenda had no control.

Gwen watched Brenda wring her hands and pace up and down the hall as she worried about every conceivable facet of the complex accounting procedure. If one of the girls input a number into the wrong G/L category, Brenda agonized about it for days. Maybe if she hadn't hired the girl in the first place, or if she'd spent more time training, or if the computer system, which she had no voice in purchasing, was more user friendly the mistake wouldn't have happened.

Brenda was a victim of her emotions . . . and most of her emotions were a complex tapestry of guilt. Over lunch one day, Gwen tried to explain guilt was another face of fear, but Brenda couldn't grasp the concept.

"Really, Brenda," Gwen offered, "you had no notice the CFO was going to change the chart of accounts over the weekend."

"But I should have anticipated--he's been talking about it for weeks," Brenda sniffed into her handkerchief.

It was her responsibility to make certain everyone in the office had the new conversion codes. She has no excuse--even if her secretary left early on Friday without emailing the change to everyone in the department. Gwen was becoming annoyed with Brenda's inability to see reason.

18

Wringing her hands, Brenda leaned over an untouched salad as they ate lunch in the EDR. "I know you're right, Gwen, but I still feel guilty. The President and CFO are mad at the entire general ledger department. Everything is in a huge mess."

"Well, if the CFO isn't having any sleepless nights over the matter, I fail to understand why you're such a nervous wreck!" Gwen wanted to shake Brenda.

"Yes, but it *was* my department that made the mistake."

Gwen felt her voice rise a full octave, the ceramic tile acted like the acoustics in an echo chamber and other people turned to stare. "*You* didn't change the codes! *Your girls* were only doing what they've been trained to do! Is that so hard to understand?"

"Intellectually I understand--but emotionally I still feel guilty." From her expression, Brenda was just as perplexed at her own behavior.

"Good grief!" Gwen threw up her hands in despair. "I'll have to get back to you on that one later."

That night, after the Jay Leno show, Gwen spun the dial on the PPM until she found Brenda's childhood frequency. It didn't take long to discover the basis of the grown woman's irrational behavior. Gwen zoomed in on a classroom, where a child was being scolded by a nun. Parochial school was cold, hard, and rigid. Most teachers were priests and nuns, who'd dedicated their lives to serving the Church. Gwen found some of their ideas contradictory. Planting concepts in fertile young minds was the prerogative of people who never had any children. Creative, independent thinking was discouraged, and information was learned by rote. While well meaning, the nuns and priests discouraged ideas which ran contrary to conventional Catholic dogma.

The PPM zoomed in on an incident which formulated much of Brenda's belief about herself; although it happened so long ago she didn't remember it. An imposing black habit leaned over a six-year-old child. Brenda labored over her picture with a fistful of crayons lying on the desk. She was concentrating hard, her nose an inch above the paper, her tongue protruding from the corner of her mouth.

The nun asked, "Brenda, what are you drawing?"

"A picture of heaven."

"Heaven? What do you know about heaven? Let me see." Like a specter rising from a dark pit, the nun extended a boney hand from the sleeve of her habit.

More than a little afraid, Brenda pushed the picture across her desk. The look on the sister's face was forbidding.

"Why, Brenda, the sky in Heaven is blue! In Heaven, the sky would never be purple, and an angel would certainly never wear a red gown! This picture is all wrong--I can't imagine where you could have gotten such a strange notion. Rip this one up. It's all wrong. Do it over again, and this time--do it right!"

To the little girl, it seemed as if the nun, whose stark white wimple framed a humorless face, represented the wrath of God, whom Brenda already learned was harsh and unforgiving. With the entire class staring at her, Brenda was so embarrassed she wished the earth would open and swallow her. It was obvious she had no artistic talent and her imagination got her in trouble. Next time, she'd know better. She would make sure the sky was blue and the angels dressed in white. The sister was still shaking her head when she returned to her desk. Brenda's picture was so bad the nun called for a second opinion, because Sister Margaret motioned for Sister Magdalene to come stand beside her with a wave.

"Have you ever seen anything like this?"

"Not in all my born days. What are you going to do?"

"Discourage that child from ever painting anything so blasphemous again. It just won't do to have angels in red--that's an exciting color and everyone know angels don't go in for anything like excitement."

"Keep a close eye on that one; she could spell trouble if the other kids decide to indulge in flights of fancy. Disciple is the key to keeping order in the classroom."

"Oh, Sister, you couldn't be more right. I'll give her an "F", that'll teach her a lesson."

Gwen moved the PPM ahead another couple of years. This time, Brenda's mother was delivering a scathing rebuke. "Brenda, for heaven sake you never think of anyone but yourself. You're the most selfish girl I've ever seen! Why wouldn't you want to take your little brother to your friend's birthday party? Do you want to be the only one to ever have fun? God knows I have to work hard all day long, but it seems too much to ask you to take your brother to a party, so I can nap."

Gwen knew Brenda *always* had to take her brother wherever she went. It didn't seem unreasonable for a ten-year-old girl to want to attend her friend's party by herself. The bricks of guilt were being piled up one by one, mortared into place by the actions and reactions of Brenda's parents and the nuns who were her teachers. Authority figures in the child's life guided Brenda with criticism and withheld praise as a form of punishment. Pleasure was prohibited because it was associated with sinful activities and God forbid Brenda ever displayed any form of what the sisters consider selfish behavior!

"You're so selfish," was a phrase Brenda's mother used like the lash of a whip. Before she reached her teens, Brenda was convinced any thoughts of self were to be rooted out like a noxious weed. Brenda was her mother's babysitter and extracurricular activities were squelched because of family responsibilities. If her mother didn't have something for Brenda to do--the nuns did. Brenda grew up thinking of herself as everyone's charwoman. At least Cinderella ended up with a handsome prince! Walls of guilt hemmed Brenda in on all sides. Wherever she turned, whatever she did, the walls were so high she couldn't see over them. Brenda was trapped between layers of resentment mortared together by guilt.

"Hmmm, what to do, what to do?" Gwen turned the question over in her mind for days and the days turned into weeks. "What to do, what to do?" It ran through her thoughts like a haunting melody. Gwen was sure Brenda would take offense if she dared point out how damaging the nuns were. And she knew for certain if she criticized Brenda's sainted mother— oh, dear, the world would collapse on Brenda forever.

"What to do, what to do? Call the Supreme Wizard? Check in with another Fairy Godmother who might have experienced such an unfortunate situation? Gwen was perplexed. How could she explain the muddled point of view Brenda accepted as the "Gospel According to Those in Authority"? Would she ever be able to make Brenda see both the nuns and her mother had purely selfish agendas aimed at keeping the young girl under their control?

After all, what if other children started seeing angels in different colored robes? What if other kids in the class thought they were worthy to have God's messengers speak to them directly? Blaspheme! Everyone knew God only spoke to the Pope! Sometimes, the Virgin Mary selected common individuals to act as Divine Spokespersons, but snotty nosed children acting out in Parochial school classrooms were never the recipients of divine inspiration. Angels dressed in red robes! Surely that was the mark of the Devil trying to gain the upper hand in Brenda's childish brain! Control--better to control the child by any means at hand--lest the Devil take possession of her soul.

The nun's thought the Devil capable of appearing at any moment, in any form, to take control of any human being weak enough to give up the spiritual fight. And dirty, smelly, sick, coughing children were singled out by the nuns as in need of discipline.

And Brenda's mother--for heaven sake, what would she do if she didn't have Brenda to help with the laundry, dishes, cooking, cleaning, and taking care of the other gaggle of children who wore her to a frazzle. It was easy to order Brenda about like a scullery maid. "Do this. Do that. Why didn't you anticipate your baby brother throwing his mashed potatoes on the floor! Well, clean them up! It's your fault for not watching him closer. And what about your little sister? She needs a bath! Get her in the tub and don't forget to wash her hair. Sissy needs to look good tomorrow, she's singing for the nuns. And look at your hair! For heaven sake, when was the last time you ran a comb through your hair?" Demands were never ending. No matter how much Brenda did, no matter how much responsibility she assumed for her mother's children--it was never enough. Nothing she did met with her mother's approval.

Like the Great Wall of China, layers of guilt spread in every direction and were piled so high they blotted out reason. Brenda couldn't see the light of day and Gwen despaired over being able to help a woman whose self-esteem seemed lower than the bottom of the Grand Canyon.

"What to do, what to do?" Suddenly, Gwen had an idea. The next day, Gwen asked Brenda to join her in the park on Sunday to attend a concert being given in the band shell. Some of the children in the Parkside Baptist Church were going to perform Negro spirituals so popular after the Civil War. Gwen knew the music reflected the deep psychological impoverishment of most former slaves. They were a battered and abused group of people who struggled to make a life for themselves. All they had to sustain them was a deep belief in a better life, and a passionate belief Jesus would lead them to a brighter day. Somehow, Gwen thought the haunting melodies, heart rending lyrics and the angelic voices of the children might strike a chord in Brenda that would bore a hole through her emotional prison. Gwen knew if she could just take a chink out of the wall Brenda had built around herself, childhood memories would begin to seep through the crack. What began as a small fissure would soon become a hole and the hole would give way to a crack in her emotional dam. When that happened, Brenda would be able to release all the childhood memories locked behind the wall of repressed memory. Once memories were released--Brenda could examine the nuns and her mother from the perspective of adulthood. She would see them as flawed human beings rather than exalted persons so much wiser, so much worthier than herself.

It was risky business; it was like taking Brenda to the bottom of

Hoover Dam and telling her to place a stick of dynamite between the large concrete slabs which held back the mighty Colorado River. But unless she got Brenda to look at the authority figures of childhood through adult eyes, her life would continue in endless cycles of reproach and remorse.

Together, they spread a blanket on a grassy spot underneath a huge Mulberry tree and Gwen opened the picnic basket she packed for the occasion. She opened a bottle of wine and handed Brenda a glass, then lifted the lid from containers filled with cold fried chicken and home-made potato salad. Brenda leaned against the tree and settled back. As the children lined up on stage beneath the band shell, Brenda finished off her first glass of wine--and Gwen refilled her glass. The conductor moved in front of the children and lifted his arms. His dark blue robe fell from his wrists like the wings of a bird as he gave the signal to begin.

A glorious sound echoed from the band shell as children began to sing at the top of their angelic lungs:

"Go down Moses
Way down to Egypt land
Tell Ole Pharaoh
To let my people go
Oppressed so hard they
Could not stand,
Let my people go"

Thunderous applause rose in a tumultuous crescendo as the children's exuberant voices filled the hillside with the last refrain of "Let My People Go." The choir master turned, bowed to the audience, and called several of the smaller children to the front of the stage. They formed an arc in front of the rest of the choir, and the littlest girl began to clap and sing in a voice that belied her size and years.

"Going home in the chariot
In the morning
Such a hard race to run,
Oh Lord, how long?"

The crowd was on its feet, swaying and clapping; spirits lifted by the song of a child whose voice carried to the gates of heaven from the middle of a desert as dry and dusty as the land Moses led his people through to the Promised Land.

"I must go and stand my trial
I got to stand it for myself

Dere's a better day a comin"

By now there was not a dry eye in the crowd; strangers reached for each other's hands. They embraced like long lost friends and sang with the choir as though the Jesus waited for them just behind the cloud on the horizon tinged with a lining of silver.

"One more river to cross
If you get there before I do
Slavery chain done broke at last
Steal Away, Steal Away, Steal Away to Jesus
Steal Away, Steal Away, I haven't got long to stay here."

As the thunderous applause began to die, the children resumed their places in the choir. The conductor lowered his arms and bowed his head. He appeared lost in thought, as if offering a silent prayer for the souls of all those gathered in the park. When his arms rose at last, every eye was on him. He looked at the children; they stared back at him, waiting for some silent, mysterious signal. With a sudden flick of his wrist, and the downward stroke of his arm, the choir burst into song. The sound carried through the park and crossed the asphalt parking lot; it moved up streets; wafted up canyons devoid of vegetation and passed over mountain peaks as bleak and haunting as the Wilderness of Judah.

"Free at last, free at last
I thank God, I'm free at last,
Me and my Jesus going to meet and talk
Thank God I'm free at last."

The crescendo softened then slowly faded away. In the distance, a lonely coyote bayed at a newly risen moon and the crowd was so filled with rapture they forgot to clap. At first, the lonely sound of one-person clapping startled the crowd. Then others joined in and before long the whole park was filled with applause which echoed the thunder of an approaching storm.

Around them, people began to pack their picnic hampers and fold the blankets spread along the ground. Brenda looked around and reached for the hamper. "No," Gwen said, "let's wait until the crowd clears out. Hand me that bottle of wine, let's finish it!"

Brenda handed Gwen the bottle of delightful Merlot, "Okay by me, I've got nowhere else to go and it is such a beautiful night. Look," she gestured at the horizon, "at all the stars."

Gwen listened to Brenda talk about Orion's Belt, the Big and Little

Dipper, and the Milky Way strung across the velvety black sky like a shower of diamonds. She reached into her pocket and withdrew the packet of fairy dust she'd brought along on impulse. Sprinkling a dusting along the top, Gwen swirled the glass of Merlot before handing it to Brenda. Then she dipped into the picnic basket and brought out a dozen homemade sugar cookies. "Dessert beneath the stars, nothing like it," Gwen commented with contentment. Before she passed the basket of cookies to Brenda, Gwen applied another layer of fairy dust on the top too. "Here, these are luscious."

Only a few stragglers remained in the park, enjoying the evening like Gwen and Brenda. Sipping their wine and nibbling on the sugar cookies, Brenda relaxed against the blanket. "Can I ask you something personal?" Gwen started the conversation she'd been planning for weeks.

"Sure, there's not much about my life worth knowing, but I'll tell you--it's the least I can do for bringing me here tonight," Brenda sighed as if she would do anything to keep the evening in the park from ending.

"Why do you always feel responsible for everything that goes wrong in the office?" Gwen kept her tone neutral to make sure Brenda wasn't offended.

"I don't know. I just do," Brenda's voice trailed away on the quickening breeze.

"Tell me about your childhood, where did you go to school?" Gwen acted casual, as if the question had no deeper purpose.

"It was boring. Catholic school, nuns, oldest in a family of five. The usual stuff." Brenda's voice was soft, as if she didn't want to think about a childhood in which she never seemed to measure up to everyone's expectations.

"Hmmm, I understand nuns can be strict."

"That's putting it mildly."

"What do you remember most?"

"About the nuns?"

"I guess, I don't know anything about that kind of school."

"There was one situation I remember."

"What happened?" Gwen remained interested, conversational, not prodding or prying.

"I remember when I drew a picture of heaven with a purple sky and an angel wearing a red robe." The breath got stuck half-way up Brenda's throat. "The sister got mad at me and made me draw a new picture. She said heaven wasn't purple and an angel would never wear a red robe. She said what I drew was sinful." Brenda's eyes were riveted on the blanket, and a film of tears frosted her lenses.

"How do you suppose the nun would know about the colors in heaven?" Gwen kept her attention trained on the stars overhead. "Do you think she'd ever been there?"

"How could she? She was still alive!" Brenda said with a note of exasperation in her voice.

"Exactly! If the nun was still alive, then she'd never seen heaven for herself. She was taking someone else's word for it, and most likely--they'd never been there either. In my opinion, your view of heaven could be valid. After all, God created every color in the rainbow, why would He exclude red or purple? I think someone on the nun's staff was confused."

"You think I might have been right?" Now it was Brenda's turn to be confused. She assumed the nuns knew everything--they were teachers who dedicated their life to the Church."

"Why not? I don't think anyone alive can really say for sure what heaven is--or is not!" Gwen passed the cookies in Brenda's direction.

"Wow, I never thought about it like that," Brenda said as she reached for another cookie without thinking.

"And--why do you think your mom was never satisfied with you?" Gwen brushed the cookie crumbs from her blouse but didn't move or act like it was time to go.

"I never understood that either. I always tried to help with my brothers and sisters. There was always so much to do around the house I had trouble getting my homework done. And then my mother got mad at me because my grades weren't good enough." Brenda offered.

"Hmmmm. Wasn't there anyone else to help your mom?"

"No, my dad left the family when all the kids were real young. My mom had to go to work and that left me to take care of all my younger siblings. Money was tight; there wasn't enough for a sitter or daycare."

"Boy, that must have been hard for your mother. "

"Yeah, real hard.  It was all she ever talked about."

"Didn't she have friends?"

"No, she said she didn't have time, energy or money for friends and all their activities."

"Sounds like she was bitter and frustrated."

"You can say that again."

Gwen thought about it for a minute, trying to decide what to say to Brenda to make the other woman realize her mother had taken out her frustration on the oldest daughter who happened to look a lot like her wayward father.  "If you'd been in your mom's situation, what do you think you would have done?"

"I don't know, I never thought about it before."  Brenda flashed a glance at Gwen; the truth was she analyzed her early childhood repeatedly.

"I'll bet you wouldn't have criticized your oldest child, you seem too soft hearted for that."  Gwen let the word linger and waited for Brenda's reaction.

"You're right, I wouldn't have been hard on my kids.  None of us were responsible for my dad's taking off and leaving us like he did.  We suffered too.  All of us thought it was our fault he left--maybe if we hadn't fought so much."  Brenda felt the all too familiar lump form in her throat.

"Where'd you get that idea?  Why would you think you and your brothers and sisters were the reason he left?"  Gwen could feel the emotional dam about to break in Brenda.

Suddenly, Brenda looked directly at Gwen, with an unfamiliar fire in her eyes.  "Because my mother told us so all the time.  Maybe we weren't responsible at all--maybe he didn't want to leave us--just my mother."  Brenda's shoulders squared.  She took a deep breath and stared hard at the horizon.

"Could be, you ought to think about that some more.  Maybe there were other things your mother said that were only true from her perspective.  Maybe your mother didn't know how to express her frustration, fear, anger-- and loneliness.  Maybe you kids had to take the brunt of her emotions because there was nowhere else for her to vent."

"I think you're right.  I think she was so bitter it clouded everything she said and did."  A new light on her childhood began to illuminate the dark corners of Brenda's emotional closet. All the baggage she had carried for so many years began to slough away--like a snake's skin in the season of molting.

Something happened inside--Brenda vowed she'd think long and hard about her childhood. She needed to put things in a new perspective, to view the actions of her mother and the scolding nuns from an adult point of view. She wasn't a child anymore and Brenda made up her mind she was going to stop acting like a little kid trying to please every adult in authority!

They left the park holding the picnic basket between them. Conversation was light, talking about how much they enjoyed the children's performance, and how incredible the evening had been. The music, the stars, the shared friendship--it was a new experience for Brenda. "Let's do this again!" Brenda gushed. "I've never had such a wonderful time. I'll look up the community concert schedule on the Internet when I get home. Can we make plans to go again?"

"I'd like that a lot," said Gwen. "I had a fantastic time too. Maybe we can get one of the other girls in the office to go with us. Someone else might enjoy the Picnic in the Park concert series if we invited them."

No matter what the future held for Brenda, Gwen knew she was "free at last, free at last." Gwen felt like skipping. Brenda was well on her way to breaking free of a past which imprisoned her behind bars of self-defeat. Brenda was going to come to terms with the way the nuns used guilt as a potent weapon in their arsenal of repression. Gwen was confident Brenda would peel back the layers of doubt and insecurity thrust on her by her mother. Yes sir, Brenda was a passenger of the train to freedom!

# CHAPTER FOUR
## *The Problem With Mikey*

**M**ikey was the youngest son in a big Italian family. All he knew was hand-me downs from parents who'd grown immune to the needs of their demanding brood because they were too poor, too defeated, and too worn down by life to think they could provide anything extra for their kids.

And their last son, poor little boy, was born with a birth defect which made him limp. There was no money to correct the situation--hell-- they couldn't afford Kleenex for a snotty nose, let alone surgery and hospitalization. Although it broke his mother's heart to see the little boy scuttling after his older brothers, with no hope of keeping pace, all she could do was insulate herself from the child's suffering. It was her fault he was deformed, she knew it...she smoked and drank throughout her pregnancy to dull the pain of poverty. There were times she couldn't look herself in the mirror. Poverty etched furrows around her eyes and mouth, her skin looked as parched and cracked as a dry lakebed in the Mojave Desert.

Born in poverty, disabled, uneducated, with no one to lend a helping hand, Mikey accepted the fate he'd been dealt with the fatalism of a loser at a 21 table. Inferiority formed the prison bars that held him captive. All he knew was how to be poor, short, crippled, and uneducated.

Gwen reflected on Mikey's conditions and decided her first plan of action was to alter the corporate medical plan! She was going to change the rules to include the surgery required to add a titanium rod to lengthen and strengthen his leg bone.

As soon Mikey returned to work after recuperating from surgery, Gwen engineered a transfer to the bar department. With his usual pluck, Mikey worked his way up to bartender and nearly doubled his salary. To make certain he had all the money he needed to continue the changes in his life, Gwen made a habit of sitting at the end of the bar during his shift. When a customer ordered a drink, she'd point her magic wand in their direction and shoot an ounce or two of fairy dust across the video poker machines recessed into the bar top. Without exception, customers always left Mikey a big tip and promised they'd be back to see him real soon!

As part of the overall "Mikey Makeover", Gwen influenced him to spend a few dollars on some decent clothing. And, as his bank account swelled, she encouraged him to purchase a sporty new car. Mikey didn't think he could afford a new car, he wasn't confident about his change in status yet, but she got him to purchase a red convertible he found on eBay with only a few thousand miles on it. Mikey got an unbelievable deal after Gwen worked a little of her magic on the guy in Phoenix selling the car, who looked dazed as the young bartender and the crazy broad drove away. There was something about the way she kept blinking her eyes at him that made him uncomfortable--that must have been why he committed to such a low-ball deal.

With some subtle encouragement, Gwen got Mikey to attend a couple of night classes at a local college. Slowly at first, and then with a rapid acceleration that surprised them both, Mikey improved his education. He soon discovered he was one smart dude and that realization super-charged his self-esteem. His Dad always made Mikey feel as though he were the dumbest of his sons. With his appearance smoothed out and his educational horizons expanding, Gwen suggested the Beverage Director take note of the up-and-coming kid behind the bar. Before long, Mikey moved into the position of shift supervisor. It wasn't long before everyone in the casino seemed to realize Mikey was a smart, hard-working young man. With a few more applications of fairy dust, he was promoted to Assistant Beverage Manager on swing-shift--where all the action and most of the money changed hands in the casino business.

Mikey didn't limp anymore. He moved out of his parent's squalid apartment and got a place of his own. The more distance he put between himself and his old man, the more confidence he gained in his own ability. And, when he stopped to think about all the things he'd accomplished in a short amount of time, Mikey began to take pride in his accomplishments.

One day as he was bustling through the basement toward the employee dining room, he almost ran over a girl who'd dropped an arm full of papers on the floor. "Oh, pardon me! I wasn't looking where I was going!"

Mikey bent down and started picking up the scattered papers. He handed them to the girl, whose badge identified her as Catherine from Accounting. She started to get up, lost control of the folder and the papers slid to the floor again. "Oh, for heaven sake," she said annoyed and embarrassed.

"Let's do it this way . . . you stand up and I'll hand you the papers." Mikey retrieved the papers from the floor and stood up, prepared to hand Catherine the pile of papers. But when he looked in her eyes, and really saw her face for the first time, his breath got stuck somewhere in the middle of his chest. Catherine Angelo was the most beautiful girl he'd ever seen. "Why don't I carry these to Accounting for you?" His voice came out higher than he wanted, but he knew he had to say something to engage her in conversation. "If they get out of order any more than they already are, you'll spend hours trying to make sense of this report," Mikey felt like he was making a fool of himself, but he couldn't let her leave.

"All right, that's nice of you. The CFO is waiting for this information, and I don't want to get reprimanded--again." Catherine couldn't imagine such a nice guy existed in the casino business. Experience made her feel as though she was a modern-day Cinderella, working day and night for people who didn't appreciate her efforts in the slightest.

"I've heard about the CFO's reputation--people call her the Wicked Witch of the West. When we get to your office, I'll help you sort the pages and put them in order. Let's not give her a reason to yell at you again." Mikey walked through the cold gray concrete tunnels with a spring in his step and a smile on his face that wouldn't fade.

He huddled over the table, helping Catherine put the pages in order, making new Xerox copies of pages gotten smudged as they lay on the concrete floor. When the report was finally in order--he knew he had to take a step, or the heavenly angel would never cross his path again. "Say, what time is your lunch break? Can I meet you in the EDR?"

Catherine stared at him, her mouth open, not knowing what to think. Most guys in the casino were only out for one thing--she'd learned that soon enough. They talked a good game, but it wasn't long before they stopped calling and then they wouldn't even glance in your direction if you crossed paths on the casino floor.

Mikey had never been so scared in all his life. He was petrified she was going to tell him no thanks, or to mind his own business, or drop dead.

There was something different about this guy, Catherine felt certain, but all her experience with casino jerks were about to rise and claim her when Gwen walked into accounting with a stack of payroll reports. "Catherine, will you please get these onto the CFO's desk? I told her I'd have them an hour ago and she's going to email my boss if they're not

31

waiting for her," Gwen's look was pleading.

"Sure, give them to me. She's been in a meeting for a couple of hours--she'll never know when they got to her desk. We do that a lot around here; it's a grand conspiracy to fool the CFO! We all work together to avoid her wrath." Catherine scooped the payroll reports from Gwen's hands and disappeared into the CFOs office.

Gwen turned to Mikey and smiled. "Isn't she just the sweetest thing you've ever seen?"

"Absolutely, Gwen, I can't believe I never ran into her before. Where's she been hiding?" Mikey's eyes never left the door, waiting for Catherine to return.

In the pocket of her skirt, Gwen rubbed the magic wand and pointed it in the direction of the CFO's office door just as Catherine returned. With any luck at all, a little of the magic dust would carry over into the CFO's office and help the disposition of one of the sourest women on the face of the planet, who seemed to want everyone else to be as unhappy as she was.

Catherine engaged Mikey with a warm smile. "It's time for me to go to lunch. When is your lunch break?"

Mikey thought he was going to float above the dingy office carpet. "Right now, as a matter of fact. I was on my way to the EDR when I almost ran over you. Come on, we'll lay plans for melting the Wicked Witch of the West with water from the office cooler!"

Gwen smiled as the two young people left the room laughing and talking about how to end the reign of terror. She'd vowed to keep an eye on the two of them and smooth their way to the altar. They both deserved a break in life and the comfort which came when two people were truly in love with each other. They'd learn to view the casino business as a means of earning a living and recognize the most important thing in life was the value they placed on each other--not the opinion of bosses, co-workers, and relatives who could be jealous of both their love for each other and success in their jobs.

Gwen decided right then and there to surround them with the golden glow only a fairy godmother could bestow on human beings. The golden glow would see them through life, sealed in the cocoon of their love for each other. The slings and arrows of other people would ricochet off into space to be dissolved into nothingness by the celestial choir assigned to helping humanity. Gwen would see to it that Catherine and Mikey became the couple everyone always admired. The man and woman who epitomized what a relationship *could* be--the couple that still enjoyed each other's company and looked at each other with love in their eyes after they'd been married fifty years.

It didn't seem to happen often enough in humans--but men and women were really meant to be together; to raise a family; to be with one another other until the very end.

# CHAPTER FIVE
## *Shelly, Shelly, Shelly*

On the heels of several consecutive successes with humans placed in her care, Gwen ran smack dab into Shelly. Oh, how she tried to stop the on-coming tide of people who made their way into Shelly's life--sucking all her time, energy, and money. Everyone wanted Shelly to do something for them. Gwen had never seen such a self-sacrificing individual in all her days on earth. Well, granted, it wasn't like she'd been born here or anything, but she was picking up speed with the human experience.

Take the office for instance. All Shelly's co-workers expected her to bring the cake for everyone's birthday. And it was up to Shelly to arrange all the office social events: picnics, the Christmas party, the Bosses day celebration, and the never-ending stream of showers--both bridal and baby! Gwen had no way to compare, but she was certain humans were the most prolific marrying and babying species in the universe based on all the showers Shelly arranged. It was amazing to Gwen how everyone conveniently forgot to pay Shelly for their share of decorations, food, and deposits on the punch bowl.

Because she was an executive assistant to the President of the Swami Hotel and Casino, co-workers and acquaintances asked her to make reservations to shows all over town--and then wanted Shelly to use her influence to get them "comped." People walked on Shelly like she was a doormat. If they got Shelly involved, no one had to put their hand in their own pocket. Shelly always took care of everything, and everyone took her kindness, skills, and self-sacrificing nature for granted.

Gwen was stumped. In sheer and utter desperation, Gwen dialed 7-1-1 and waited for the Supreme Wizard to pick up. Fresh from her success with Mikey, Brenda and Trish, Gwen was reluctant to call on the Supreme Wizard for help, but she had no idea how to stop Shelly from being everyone's dumping ground.

Finally, the Supreme Wizard answered. It sounded like he'd been taking a nap. When Gwen finished explaining Shelly's situation, the Supreme Wizard settled back on his star-studded throne. He studied Gwen on the PPM screen. Then he cocked his head, deciding to give her some advice. Normally, he didn't help fairy godmothers out of their muddle, but he decided it was time to test Gwen, to see if she was really on the way to the coveted position of Guardian Angel.

"Well, it's clear there's only one thing to do," The Supreme Wizard said to Gwen via the marvel of the PPM speaker phone.

"Oh, thank you for helping. I knew you'd know what is best for Shelly. I just haven't been able to figure it out." As Gwen waited for the revelation, she hardly remembered to breathe.

"Have her fired. It will solve all her problems," the Supreme Wizard said with authority. Then the screen went black--he'd hung up.

"Wait! Wait a minute! Come back! That's the most awful thing I've ever heard! That's no answer at all." Gwen felt like she was going to have a seizure. She started to dial his emergency number again but thought better of it. Once the Supreme Wizard spoke it was all over. Whining and complaining weren't going to get her anywhere. But, but whatever was he thinking? For the first time since she set upon the path of fairy sprite-- Gwen was losing faith herself, and fairies, and angels, and--and, even the Supreme Wizard.

Gwen sat on the swing in the backyard, or at least what passed for a backyard in the middle of the Mojave Desert and began to rock back and forth. She had to think about things. Fire Shelly? She just couldn't figure out how that was going to help. Shelly's entire sense of self-esteem came from her job. She'd worked her way up from a clerk in the Accounts Receivable Department to the Executive Assistant to the President of one of the most successful hotel/casinos on the Las Vegas Strip. Get her fired? For what--putting in too many hours?

"Oh muddle, muddle, muddle," Gwen thought. Even if it was going to be good for her, as the Supreme Wizard said, Shelly had an unblemished employment record--why would she be terminated?

"Double muddle, double muddle," Gwen muttered under her breath. She thought, and thought, and thought. Finally, from out of the blue, an idea came to Gwen. She wasn't sure if it would work, but it was the only thing she'd come up with after hours of thinking. Shelly was loyal to her boss. If someone in HR found out about all the influence peddling the President did on behalf of his friends it was grounds for termination--

the President's termination. If the President got fired, Shelly would go too through no fault of her own. No incoming President wanted to be stuck with an executive assistant with a known loyalty to the predecessor, and everyone wanted their own entourage parading around after them. Gwen knew Shelly would be cast aside like an old shoe.

Over the course of the next few weeks, Gwen flagged emails from the President to several of his friends. With the help of some fairy dust the emails ended up in the mailbox of the VP of HR, whose sworn duty it was to uphold the company's Code of Ethics. Oh, everyone knew the big bosses paid little attention to the Code, but it was there, in place, on the shelf, for it to be run out in front of politicians, reporters, and civic officials if it ever needed. Mostly, the Code was used to get rid of people they didn't want around anymore. The Code was like a religious holiday. People went to church on Easter and Christmas, so they could say they were good churchgoers. The Code made the company feel good too--it allowed the Board of Directors to pat themselves on the back about how they were fulfilling their moral obligation to the community. If it hadn't been so ludicrous it might have been humorous.

As soon as the VP of HR read the President's emails, he was on the phone to his boss--the EX VP of Corporate HR. Gwen smiled when she realized it never crossed the VP of HR's mind how the emails got into his inbox; he was far too busy counting all the violations to the Code.

The EX VP of Corporate HR went running to the CEOs office, the Code book under his arm. "He'll have to go! We can't have this . . . it's against the Code!" the EX VP bellowed.

The CEO looked depressed. The President had worked for him several years and if the truth be known his Code violations were probably no more than anyone else in the company. It's just that when these things came to light, well, the company had to act on them. If the President wasn't held up as an example to all other property Presidents, someone might leak to the Security and Exchange Commission things weren't right within the company. Couldn't afford that! No sir, scrutiny from the Feds was the last thing the CEO wanted. "Okay, get busy and process him out. Take his keys right now, cut off access to his computer, and get him off property before he has a chance to talk to anyone. If the press gets wind of it--tell them he's on administrative leave. We'll tidy up his termination and then he can fend for himself when nosey reporters find out he's no longer with the company."

The EX VP of Corporate HR rushed out of the office, dialing the head of Security as he ran back to valet parking. He waited for his black

Escalade to be brought around, then screeched out of the porte cochere as he rushed toward the Swami Hotel and Casino. This was going to send a shock wave through the Swami, the company, and the community. His mind was racing as fast as his tires were spinning while he tried to figure out how he was going to spin this firing. "Family matters," he finally decided. "Better to make everyone think his wife was ill and he'd decided to spend more time at home with her," he whispered under his breath. Not that anyone would believe the story--the President and his wife settled into a marriage of convenience a long time ago.

So, the President was called at home and told not to come back to the hotel. The VP of Security went to his house and picked up his office keys, his security access code, and the preliminary copy of the annual report. It was all over in five minutes and the former President of the Swami Hotel and Casino sat in stunned silence beneath the sun umbrella beside his pool.

Shelly had just walked into the office and turned on her computer when the VP of Security and the VP of HR burst through the office door. "Hi, Mr. Delancey; Mr. Rathbone." She was so busy going through the morning routine she'd performed for years, taking the phone off voice mail, logging on to her computer, flicking her eyes over the stack of mail--she just assumed they were here for a meeting with the President although she hadn't checked his electronic calendar yet.

"That's funny, I can't log on. I wonder if IS upgraded the system again. I'll have to call the Help Desk."

"No, Shelly, you've been locked out of the system. The President is on permanent administrative leave, and we are terminating you now. I need your keys to the office," the VP of HR stuck out one hand for the keys and put a pile of papers in front of Shelly.

"What's this? I don't get it. The President? Gone? Why? And I'm being fired? You've got to be kidding!" Shelly's voice rose several octaves as the realization of what was happening sunk in. Over the years she'd watched a lot of people get fired. Important people. Unimportant people. It was always the same. Here one minute and gone the next. All trace of their existence wiped out of company records, and human memory as well. It was best the person's name was never mentioned again. If you spoke about them, it marked you as the next person on that nefarious list which always seemed to loom somewhere in the background, ready to pounce, ready to swallow up both innocent and guilty in its sticky black tide.

"You'll get six months' severance pay. That's more than a fair settlement if you sign the Voluntary Separation Statement," the VP of HR looked down a long, thin nose at the stunned young woman.

"But, but, I haven't done anything! I've been an exemplary employee for 15 years. Why am I being fired?"

"Clean sweep", the VP of Security said. "Clean out your desk, an officer will be here to escort you to your car any minute now."

Shelly signed the Voluntary Separation Statement, she didn't have much money saved; she needed six months' severance to survive. That's the way they did it in the casino business--they got rid of you with money because they knew you could be bought off; that you'd go willingly off the end of the plank never to be seen or heard from again if you got enough money. Woodenly, she took pictures of her nieces and nephews, her cats, and the softball team which took first place in the Corporate Challenge and placed them in the box the VP of Security handed her. There wasn't much else, a tube of lipstick, a service pin for 15 years at the Swami Hotel and Casino, a rolodex with the names and phone numbers of a lot of important people in the State of Nevada.

"You can't take that," said the VP of HR.

"Oh yes I can, the rolodex is mine! All those names and addresses are handwritten—by me. That makes it my private property. You can lock up the address book in my computer, but the rolodex is mine and I'm taking it with me. You know the rule Mr. Rathbone, and you know that I know it."

From somewhere deep inside, Shelly found the will to resist. She straightened her spine and lifted her head. "Do you want to search my purse for pens and pencils too? You better make sure I'm not making off with any of the company's assets or the CFO will be down your throat this afternoon." Shelly picked up her sweater and left the office, calling back over her shoulder. "Don't worry, I can find my way to my car . . . unless you want to search my trunk!"

The VP of HR and the VP of Security were surprised at Shelly's spunk. They expected her to slink off the way most people did, embarrassed, ashamed, afraid of what the future held. They looked at each other, then glanced back to watch Shelly's retreating form. It was a good thing she didn't have the money for legal fees to start a Wrongful Termination suit—because the VP of HR knew she'd win.

Gwen watched Shelly through the PPM. She sobbed and sobbed

and sobbed. And just when she thought there were no more tears of rage to be shed, tears of sadness, despair and desolation took over. Gwen felt awful. Yet she knew the weeks ahead were going to be even harder. Part of the Supreme Wizard's scheme was to keep Shelly from finding another executive assistant position.

After being turned down for the fifth time, Shelly was so demoralized she could hardly keep the car on the road. The separation money was running out, she'd have to take an entry level position to pay her rent. Finally, she took a job as a secretary in the housekeeping department at a small, downtown hotel. It wasn't much, but it was a place to go and in ninety days she'd be covered by insurance again. Once her so-called "friends" found out she'd taken a position with no influence, they stopped calling all together. Gwen was the only person who continued to ask her to go to lunch or an occasional movie.

After months of emotional suffering, an amazing thing happened. Shelly found co-workers in her new office were drawn to her although she had nothing to offer--other than friendship. Her warm, outgoing, compassionate nature attracted fellow employees like a magnate. As the number of new friends grew, so did her self-esteem.

Gwen thought she was going to burst with pride when, shortly after being promoted to Director of VIP Services—a tactical move on Gwen's part--one of Shelly's old friends called. They'd heard about her recent promotion and wondered if she could get them comped into the new show that was opening at the Wynn. Politely, but firmly, Shelly told the used-to-be friend that she was not going to make reservations, let alone see to it they didn't have to pay. Not one word of apology, not one excuse, not a 'let me try to see what I can do'. Shelly just said no. And that was that. Gwen threw her PPM into the air and let out a whoop, which startled everyone in the office.

Hooray! Double Hooray! Shelly's confidence was growing. She'd learned real friendship was not purchased with bribes, gifts or by being a convenient doormat. Real friendship was free--no strings attached. Shelly was on her way to becoming the kind of person people liked to be around because she cared about herself as well as others. Gwen was confident things were going to be different for Shelly from now on.

About the time this realization blossomed into full flower, the PPM began to ring. "Hello?"

"Ah, Gwen, how are things going down on Planet Earth?" The Supreme Wizard seemed concerned.

"Oh, Supreme Wizard, better than I ever imagined. I doubted you, I really did, when you told me to get Shelly fired. But you were right! It was hard for Shelly at first, I thought she was never going to stop crying, but she stood up to one of her smarmy friends today and refused to get them into the newest show on The Strip for free. She didn't even apologize . . . she just said no. "Oh, Supreme Wizard, I can't thank you enough for the advice," Gwen knew she was babbling but just couldn't seem to stop.

"So, I was right after all?" The humor oozed from the Supreme Wizard's voice.

"Oh yes, and now I'm sorry I ever doubted you. You're always right." Gwen thought she was going to burst into tears because she was embarrassed by her lack of faith in someone whose intentions always had everyone's best interest at heart. "I'm sorry, will you forgive me?" Gwen started to blubber.

"Oh, Gwen, I'll have none of that. Life on earth is harder than in Golfinsphere. Everything must be learned by experience, and often those experiences are painful. You set Shelly on the right path, and I'm proud of you."

"You are?" Gwen didn't see why the Supreme Wizard would be proud of her.

"Absolutely! You followed my advice, even though it hurt you to cause Shelly so much pain. You're starting to like your humans, but you never deviated from the path. And now you've learned that even though change was hard for Shelly, she's a much better person today than she was six months ago. All because of you Gwen, and the courage it took to see your friend suffer." The Supreme Wizard was so pleased with Gwen his eyes were all a twinkle as he hung up the PPM.

"Well, I'll be." And Gwen headed out the office door humming the tune from a tuna fish commercial with a smile on her face which blazed as brightly as the noon day sun.

# CHAPTER SIX
## *Gilda, Where Have All the Flowers Gone?*

Gilda was a living example of just how far well-intended human beings had muddied up the Supreme Wizard's simple rules. Her mother, a somber woman, who usually dressed in depressing black, gave Gilda an entirely wrong impression about the Supreme Wizard--and what he wanted from her. She made Gilda think she was a bad person because she got mad at her little brother for doing all the horrible things little brothers are known to do. The misguided woman made Gilda feel guilty about her all too human emotions and the poor girl decided early in life she was doomed to failure because she kept breaking all the rules

Gilda's marriage ended in divorce. Her children seldom called, and her pesky little brother grew up to be an indifferent human being. So, Gilda plodded through life, afraid social interaction would cause her to accrue still more black marks against her in the Supreme Wizard's Book of Books. Gwen clucked her tongue. Gilda was going to be a challenging case. Righting an attitude that held the poor woman prisoner for over fifty years was going to take a lot of effort!

The few people in the office who knew Gilda well said she felt guilty about World War II because she happened to be born the same year the Nazis invaded Poland. Gilda was taught it was a sin not to strive for perfection. The mental yardstick by which Gilda measured not only herself but every other human being with whom she had interaction was supposed to follow these same rigid and inflexible as the Rock of Gibraltar rules. Every woman should care for her children--just right. And, they had to cook and clean--just right. Children had to be neat, clean, respectful, and well groomed; they had to speak when spoken to and they were never supposed to voice an opinion. Children, well, children had to be--just right.

Co-workers were supposed to be punctual, dedicated, self-sacrificing, willing to take on more and more responsibility. They had to fit the company model of a good worker and they had to volunteer their time, energy, and money to all the lofty goals which made certain the community thought the Swami Hotel and Casino was a good corporate citizen. All the employees in her department had to work diligently, never take breaks, never linger at the coffee pot, never engage in lengthy conversations with their office mates, never gossip or complain about the bosses, why--they had to be just right.

Gilda went through her day peering over her glasses toward the receptionist if the call wasn't picked up on the second ring. She cleared her throat loudly if the conversation in the next cubicle went on too long. There were also times when she had to stand with her hands on her hips and snort at the younger girls, so they would get back to work. What was this younger generation coming to? All they did was talk about the latest antics of one rock star or another. Where were their brains? As far as Gilda was concerned the combined mental acumen of the young women in her section wouldn't fill a teaspoon. What to wear, who to date, who was going to what concert, what was happening to friends on Facebook, who saw the latest video on YouTube --good grief, there wasn't a single syllable of intelligent conversation amongst all the young girls who looked like overgrown Barbie dolls.

Gilda sighed. Her kids got mad at her because she was constantly pushing them to achieve. Sports, academics, school government, community involvement-- push, push, push, push, push. Her kids got out of the house as soon as they found jobs. Why didn't they see their lives would be so much better if they tried harder? Gilda just didn't understand the younger generation. They were, well, they were just all wrong.

Gwen watched Gilda from afar for several weeks. She was as stern and unforgiving as the mother she outwardly revered. Although Gilda didn't recognize the similarity between herself and her mother, it was as though she'd turned into a younger model of a shriveled up old woman, desperately unhappy, tired, and bitter.

What to do, what to do, what to do? Gwen didn't want to turn to the Supreme Wizard again. He was going to think she was incapable of helping her humans without His direction. Well, maybe she was--maybe she had no business trying to become a fairy godmother. Gwen sunk into as deep a funk as Gilda, which was very unlike a young sprite from Golfinsphere.

What to do, what to do, what to do? Gwen peered through the PPM as Gilda hunched over her computer screen trying to figure out why all the numbers didn't balance. Oh, it was so frustrating! Someone input something wrong, and Gilda was losing patience with the entire project. Just then, the comptroller strolled over to her desk. He could tell by the clouded look on Gilda's face something was wrong with the best Accounts Payable supervisor he'd ever had. "Gilda, what's the matter?" His tone was soft and gently inquiring. He didn't want to put her on the defensive--that happened one time and it had taken weeks to gain her confidence back.

"I can't make this report balance! I've been at it since early this morning, and I've gone over it again and again." Her mood was as bleak as the far side of the moon.

"Let me take a look at it." He scrolled down the computer screen and then tabbed across several columns. "Here, look at this. Missy input this column twice! No wonder you couldn't get it to work out." The controller leaned over her desk, careful not to get too far into her personal space, but close enough to read the computer screen which was growing harder to see all the time.

"Good grief! Why didn't I see that?" Gilda was flustered and embarrassed.

"Well, probably because you've been putting in way too many hours and you're worn out. It happens all the time. You need some time off--a little R and R," a gentle smile warmed his face. "When was the last time you did something fun?"

Gilda was perplexed. "Fun?"

"Yes, what do you like to do for fun?"

"I don't think I ever thought about it before. Fun?" There was a far-away tone in her voice like the concept was so foreign she didn't even know how to respond.

As Gwen watched the interaction from afar; a glimmer of an idea began to form somewhere in the back of her mind. "Hmmm," she thought, "I wonder . . . ." Gwen skipped out of the office, pleased she'd thought of a solution without calling the Supreme Wizard for advice.

The very next day, Gwen dropped by Gilda's desk. "Hi, Gilda, how are you?"

"Better now that I finished the report for Mr. Martin. I was really worried yesterday because I know he's waiting on these numbers. He's got a big meeting with the Corporate CFO, and I didn't want to disappoint him." Gilda tried to smile a little.

"Do you like working for Mr. Martin?"

"He's the best boss I've ever had. He's so patient--and, kind."

"I think he appreciates you too."

"You do?" Gilda flushed red to the roots of her hair.

"Yes, I do. I think he knows you're responsible and dedicated, and one heck of a nice woman." Gwen knew she was on the right track now for absolute certain.

The very next day, Gwen sprinkled some fairy dust on the report Mr. Martin, the comptroller, had to send to the Corporate CFO. It was perfect, and Mr. Martin, Ben to his peers, was proud of the job Gilda did on the report. He decided to tell her what a terrific job she'd done right then and there.

He strolled through the office and stopped at Gilda's desk. "Gilda, I just wanted to tell you what a fantastic job you did on this report. I'm sure the Corporate CFO is going to be impressed."

Gilda was stunned and didn't know how to respond. She'd been preparing this annual report on the overall financial condition of the Swami Hotel and Casino for several years and this was the first time Mr. Martin seemed to notice. "Uh...thanks."

"Gilda, how long have we been working together now?"

"Over five years."

"And I never once told you how good you make me look, have I?"

"No, Mr. Martin, you've never said that before."

"Well, Gilda, I'm here to apologize for a serious oversight. You always make me look good because we have the best financials in the company--I appreciate your efforts, and" his breath stopped half-way up his throat as he heard the words which seemed to come out of his mouth from nowhere, "and I appreciate you, more than I can say."

As he turned to walk back into his office, Gilda couldn't get her mouth to close. All she could think of to do was to turn back to the computer screen and pound the keyboard.

Ben Martin closed the door behind him and leaned against the wall. What on earth had come over him? He'd admired Gilda for a long time, but this was the workplace. He'd been to all the management classes which filled supervisors and above with fear over any kind of personal interaction with employees. Yet, he felt drawn to Gilda in a strange new way. He glanced out the office window toward her, and felt his heartbeat quicken. Something he didn't understand was happening and he no longer cared about all the rules and regulations governing conduct in the office.

Gilda went home that night with a new lightness in her step. She was humming as she put her keys and purse down on the hall table. Suddenly, the phone began to ring. It was probably just another telemarketer trying to sell some credit card fraud program, but she picked up the phone anyway. There was a slight haze of golden dust on the table, and she wiped it away with her hand before she spoke into the receiver. "Hello?"

"Gilda, hi, how are you? This is Ben."

Gilda put her hand to her mouth and breathed in the sprinkling of fairy dust Gwen deposited on the phone and hall table the night before. "Oh, I hope there's nothing wrong with the report? Do you need me to come back to the office?"

"No, Gilda, that's not why I'm calling."

"Is something else wrong?" Gilda didn't know what to think. Mr. Martin had never called her at home before.

"Well, gosh, this probably seems sudden, but I was wondering if you'd have dinner with me sometime?"

Gilda put her hand to her mouth again and breathed a big gulp of air, so surprised she couldn't even think. Then, the words seemed to tumble out of her mouth as if they had a life of their own and she wasn't in control, "I'd absolutely love to go to dinner with you--when?"

"How about tomorrow night? I know a great Mexican restaurant on the east side of town. Do you like Mexican, we can always go somewhere else if you'd like sushi, or Thai, or a steak . . . ?" His words hung in the air, he couldn't breathe; he thought his heart had quit beating as he waited for her answer.

"I love Mexican better than any other cuisine. That would be great. Do you want me to meet you there?"

"No, I'd like to pick you up at your house. That way we can talk in the car on the drive. There's a lot I want to learn about you--other than you're the best Accounts Payable supervisor in the business. How about seven tomorrow night?"

"Great! I look forward to having dinner with you." Gilda could hardly believe what just transpired. She'd always admired Mr. Martin, Ben, but thought he was out of reach. After all, he was upper management, and she was just a supervisor. But he'd called her the best supervisor in the business, and that was just about the nicest compliment she ever remembered receiving.

Gwen was gloating as she shut down the PPM. Maybe if someone she admired paid attention to her, Gilda would pay attention to herself. She had a lot of great qualities, but Gilda didn't recognize any of them because she was so hard on herself. Maybe that's why she was so demanding of others--and the revelation burst upon Gwen like the sun coming from behind a cloud. "Why, that's it! Gilda expects so much of herself it's impossible to live up to her own standards. She keeps trying, but never cuts herself any slack. Gilda thinks she needs to be a saint, and humans aren't saints--they're just human!

Gwen decided she was going to make sure Gilda relaxed her standards. She was creating a self-imposed exile from family and friends. No one expected her to be perfect and others were going to accept her imperfections, but Gwen had to make Gilda see she needed to live with other people's characteristics which were not always going to measure up to her standards.

With a twinkle in her eye, Gwen felt certain Ben was going to have a lot to do with helping Gilda accept other people just as they were.

# CHAPTER SEVEN
## *Paul – Is An Arrogant Man*

As Paul Johnson swaggered toward the coffee pot, Gwen reached for her PPM and pointed it in his direction. The arrogant casino pit boss leered at Trish, who challenged him with a disdaining glance. "What are you staring at, buster?"

"I'm the man who can make you smile," Paul answered, honey oozing through his voice.

"Not if your life depended on it!" Her retort was acid and her expression sour.

"Wanna make a bet on how fast I can make your knees knock?" Paul's hand was steady as he poured coffee into an expensive china cup, but his eyes were cold and flat--almost reptilian.

"All you can make me do is vomit!" Trish glided past the outstretched hand reaching for her perky little fanny. "Try that and I'll be in the HR office before you finish that coffee, you creep."

"Just wait . . . just wait!" Paul was concentrating on Trish's retreating form when Judith appeared at the cocktail station to get a drink for some customers in the high limit area. "Well, don't you look pretty today?" A practiced glance made it easy to imagine what the blond cocktail waitress would look like wearing a sexy little black dress instead of a tacky uniform.

"Thanks, Mr. Johnson. It's nice of you to notice." Judith was revolted, but she had two kids at home she was trying to raise by herself. Ever since her husband ran off with a dealer half his age things had been rough. She couldn't afford to alienate a big casino boss, so she smiled dutifully, batted her lashes, and prayed he wouldn't ask her to meet him for drinks when her shift was over. It was like walking a tight rope to maintain the delicate balance between friendliness and an attitude which let all the pit bosses know you weren't going to let them get to first base. If she used enough tact, maybe Mr. Johnson would let her work the pit more often.

Table game customers always tipped better than slot players, maybe because the stakes were higher, maybe because they had more class.

Most people thought Paul Johnson was one of the most self-assured men in the kingdom of gaming. But as Gwen watched him adjust the knot in his tie, smooth his hair, turn the ring on his little finger so the two-carat diamond faced the nervous cocktail waitress, she decided he was filled with anxiety. Why, for heaven sake? He had an excellent job with the largest gaming corporation in the country; he had plenty of money; and excellent health. If she asked him what was wrong with his life, Paul Johnson would wave her away with a sneer. Discretely, Gwen removed the PPM from her pocket and aimed it at the pit boss. The screen blocked out the antics of the dice players and the racket being made by the all the wannabes gawking at a high-stakes game of roulette. Gwen focused her full powers of concentrate on the pit boss. He adjusted his cuff links and patted his hair--again. Every few minutes, he would cock his foot behind his knee and rub his shoe up and down his leg, wiping imaginary dust from a leather surface so polished Gwen was certain he could use it as a mirror. Paul Johnson surveyed his domain, and the women in it, offering loud, lewd remarks and leering stares--the casino pit boss was a man always on the make.

"Is there something wrong with his libido?" Gwen wondered. "Is he trying to prove he's a man? To whom," she mused as he leaned closer to the cocktail waitress, "himself?"

Gwen pressed the zoom button and the screen filled with Paul's eyes. They were unhappy eyes, anxious eyes. He made certain every attractive woman in the casino noticed him. Searching her memory for something, anything, to give her a clue to Paul's problem, Gwen found herself at a loss. After a few nights spent downloading all the information on human beings in the extensive library at Universal "U", Gwen concluded Paul was afraid of growing old. His hair was beginning to gray, and he seemed unable to get rid of the roll around his middle which became as uncontrollable as the tide. Like an aging stallion defending his paddock against younger, stronger males, Gwen decided Paul was fighting to preserve the image he had of himself. He refused to relinquish his position of dominance in the pit or assume the role of mentor to young stallions struggling to learn the nuances of becoming an executive in a business with no product or service. It was a mystery to Gwen why people liked to put their hard-earned money on a horse, a fight, the turn of a card, toss of the dice, or the spin of a slot or roulette wheel. Gwen liked to go home with something in a shopping bag if she was going to part with the money that was so difficult to come by on planet Earth. There were always so many expenses! Rent, power, water, food, a car, and now the cost of gas was skyrocketing. Although Gwen didn't get it, thousands of people continued to pour into Las Vegas with the hope they'd go back to their humdrum lives a little richer. Sure, she thought to herself, these elaborate palaces were built by sending people back home as millionaires! A few got rich in Las Vegas, but computer programs made sure it wasn't the poor schmucks at the slots and tables. Property presidents, CEOs, the upper echelon of casino management were like well-fed cattle in the middle of a grassy paddock wondering why faces on the other side of the pasture fence seemed so bleak; why there was such a desperate look in their eyes. Paul was a classic example of casino arrogance. It never seemed to occur to him other people didn't live in the lap of luxury like he did.

Gwen watched the war rage inside Paul every time a pretty girl noticed one of the younger guys. He *was* consumed by his fear of getting old and he was oblivious to anyone else's feelings. Gwen knew she owed it to everyone to add Paul to her list. She needed to teach him growing old and dying were an inescapable part of the human equation! Why everyone and everything had an expiration date! Didn't everyone know that?

Hmmmm.....hmmmm....hmmmm, what to do, what to do? How was she going to teach Paul there were more important things in life than seducing younger women? If only he had any idea how lucky he was, how many more opportunities and possessions he had in his life than, well, a child in India, or even a family scratching by in the slums of North Las Vegas. Gwen knew Paul couldn't relate to the condition of a child growing up in a third world country or an African American family struggling to keep their kids away from the Crips and Bloods. What to do, what to do? This was a tough one and she was determined to figure it out all by herself.

A couple of weeks later, Gwen happened to be watching Paul through the PPM device as he staggered to his car. It was late, he'd put in several hours over time and had stopped off at the bar for a drink to unwind. One drink led to another, and before long he was in no condition to drive. But Paul wasn't worried. Half the judges on the bench were put there by casinos and they knew where their bread was buttered. If he got stopped, his attorney would smooth things over with a phone call and a political donation to the judge in charge of his case. After several tries, Paul finally got the keys in the door and slid behind the wheel. He was way too tired to drive, and his hand shook as he tried to shove the key into the ignition.

Rubbing his eyes with the back of his fist, Paul stared at the traffic light. When it turned green, he eased into traffic. He wasn't foolish enough to speed tonight. It was hard to concentrate and the lines on the road kept moving before his eyes. He was having a tough time staying in his lane. To his dismay, red lights started flashing and with a groan, he eased into the closest parking lot, so he didn't impede traffic.

The officer was nice, but Paul knew he reeked and wasn't surprised when he was handcuffed and led to the patrol car. Paul still wasn't worried; his attorney had gotten him out of more than one DUI.

Awakened from a sound sleep, the attorney told Paul not to worry. He posted bail with a bondsman who worked his cases and was on call 24 hours a day, seven days a week. Within an hour, Paul's attorney had him sprung from jail and delivered him to the front door of his condo. "Don't worry, Paul, I'll get this straightened out in the morning. Can you make it to bed?"

"Oh sure, Dan, and thanks. I'm sober now."

"Okay then, I'll talk to you in the morning."

It was almost noon when the attorney awakened Paul from an alcohol induced sleep. "Buddy, I'm afraid I've got terrible news."

Paul tried to concentrate--but his head was spinning, and his stomach felt like he was deep sea fishing in Alaska. "What's the matter, Dan?"

"You've been assigned to appear before Judge Helen Wilson--the hanging judge--anyway that's what most of my fellow attorneys call her. Helen Wilson has it for casino bosses, who think money and status put them above the law."

"The Hanging Judge? What the heck does that mean?" Paul's throat was dry, and his hands were shaking.

"Judge Wilson doesn't accept campaign contributions from businesses, especially casinos. She wants to make certain she remains fair and impartial. So, you'll have to appear before her--but I must warn you there's no way to make your DUI go away."

Paul stared at the phone like it was something he'd never seen before--like his attorney started speaking in tongues or something equally weird. "You're kidding . . . aren't you?"

"No, I wish I was. I'll have my secretary call you to let you know when and where to show up for your court appearance. And, Paul, a word of warning, expect to spend time doing community service. It's her trademark."

Paul felt his heart hit the floor. Good grief, a DUI that couldn't be fixed—and do community service? He'd be the laughingstock of the entire casino. No one in his position ever did community service! He wasn't about to start wiping the noses of some snotty nosed kids in North Las Vegas. And he sure in hell wasn't going to slop soup to the homeless down at the mission. His attorney would have to get the case reassigned. With that comforting thought, Paul flopped back against the bed and returned to the comforting folds of sleep.

Six months? Six months of public service--why did he pay his attorney such an enormous amount of money? He was supposed to fix things--not look woebegone as the judge brought the gavel down and thundered out a sentence with a murderous look which left no doubt an appeal would get him nowhere.

The judge had a whole list of things Paul was going to do. His first month was spent in the emergency room at the county hospital, University Medical Center, out on West Charleston. He had to help orderlies unload ambulances. Maimed and mangled flesh became common place. Paul had no idea the human body contained so much blood--a lot of it got sloshed on his highly polished Italian loafers. Drug addicts, prostitutes, the homeless, abused children, shooting and knife victims poured through the emergency room doors like the floodwaters of the river Nile. Automobile accidents were his special assignment. He was forced to hold an accident victim's hand and listen to their screams as they were rushed into the operating room in a desperate attempt to overcome the impact thousands of pounds of steel had on human flesh. When a six-month-old baby boy, severely injured in a car crash because his parents couldn't afford a car seat, died in his arms--Paul fainted. After he revived, Paul had to tell the mother, who was in a body cast from her shoulder to her knees, her baby didn't make it. The mother's wail pierced his heart and Paul never felt more helpless in his entire life. Nothing he could do, nothing he could say, would restore the frantic woman's baby. Paul left the hospital that night feeling the weight of the world pressing on his shoulders.

His next assignment was a stint at a homeless shelter down on Main. The manager made him listen to tales of woe that would have been unimaginable only weeks before. Pitiful stories about people who lost their jobs and ended up on the street were more common than casino chips in Las Vegas. The flotsam and jetsam of society passed through the shelter and ever so slowly, Paul's arrogance began to slough away like a snake's skin. He began to realize not everyone enjoyed his privilege and good fortune. For the first time in his life, Paul began to perceive circumstance laid a heavy hand on some--while sparing others--and be began to feel

51

grateful.

Gwen was worried about Paul's next assignment. The department of corrections was not a pretty place. As an assistant case worker, Paul became involved with society's outcasts. Hardened criminals, men strung out on drugs, crooks, pathological liars, cold- blooded killers, child molesters, wife beaters and petty thieves all took shots at breaking apart Paul's well-ordered world.

Listening to the case worker's lament, Paul realized most of these guys were doomed from the start. Few were raised with both parents. Most suffered from the effects of poverty. It seemed like they'd all learned to survive on the street when they were hardly more than toddlers. Despite abhorrence of their crimes, the case worker made Paul a by-stander on the terrible road which led these men to prison. Paul was horrified. He had no idea people grew up in such emotional, financial, and spiritual deprivation. The idea that most criminals deserved what they got began to soften as the sands of illusion eroded before the relentless tide of reality. Paul gained new respect for the philosophical category he'd disdained for years--a bleeding heart liberal. The rigid mindset dividing everything into black and white suddenly faded into a multitude of shades of gray. He began to realize many people were hapless victim of circumstances which shaped their lives as certainly as rain created the canyons in the Colorado River.

When he was sent to the insane asylum for a month, Paul was sure he was going to become as crazy as the inmates. He saw frantic people claw at walls because they were convinced giant bugs perused them. He helped nurses' massage withered muscles on a man whose mind was so cemented by despair he curled up into the fetal position five years ago and never moved again. Paul couldn't believe the torment in many of the inmate's eyes. Whether the cause of their psychosis was real or imagined, emotional pain was just the same. Paul was a changed man by the time he left the asylum.

His last month of public service was spent at a hospice. There, Paul stood as a silent witness to the physical suffering of terminal patients and the emotional suffering endured by grief-stricken families. He held the hands of the dying and saw several through the last moments of their life. Hours spent with those who welcomed death as a release from their pain fashioned the new man Paul was on the way to becoming.

The man who stood before Judge Wilson at the end of his community service sentence looked at the world through different eyes. Arrogance vanished and in its stead, tears of humility could not be kept in check as Paul told the Judge about his experiences.

When he returned to work in the casino, Paul used his position to help some of the men he'd gotten to know in prison find jobs in the kitchens and housekeeping department of the sprawling hotel. He kept in touch with the widows and widowers he'd met at the hospice and tried his best to help them through the roughest months of their grief. Paul championed a fund-raising event to clean up the asylum with a fresh coat of paint, and he purchased flowered bedspreads for the entire hospital. He looked at his wife through newly christened eyes and found a woman worth loving again. With his change of attitude came a sense of self- esteem which was simply amazing. Paul was no longer obsessed with himself, instead he found happiness in the one thing guaranteed to bring unlimited joy--service to others.

# CHAPTER EIGHT
## *Gwen Earns An Angelship*

The Supreme Wizard sent for Gwen. At the appointed day and time, Gwen sat in his outer chamber. She was so nervous, she was perspiring all over her PPM. She chewed her lip so much it looked as though she'd spent the last six hours in the ring with Mike Tyson. When one of the angelic hosts assigned to the waiting room finally called her name, Gwen didn't even hear the sweet, melodic voice. She jumped when the host tapped her on the shoulder.

In the audience room, Gwen stood before the Supreme Wizard, seated on his star-studded throne. He asked her to report on the outcome of her human salvage assignments. Gwen happily described each of their problems and the solutions which remedied their human muddles.

Pleased, the Supreme Wizard asked Gwen where she would like to locate and set up an Angel Dealership. Gwen bit her lip and thought about it for a minute. Finally, she replied what she really wanted was to return to earth as a fairy godmother--because that was where she could do the most good. While all the fancy trappings that went with an Angelship, like celestial music, and fabulous feathered wings were appealing, Gwen knew in her heart those things just didn't matter anymore.

With a smile so bright it crystalized the sunshine streaming into the throne room, the Supreme Wizard congratulated Gwen. He told her she passed the final test. Gwen was confused and had no idea what was going on. The Supreme Wizard explained no one ever received an Angelship unless they asked to remain on earth as a fairy godmother.

Developing a love for human beings despite all their frailties was the ultimate test--and Gwen passed with flying colors. Taking nothing but her magic wand and PPM, Gwen flapped her newly sprouted, feathered wings and hurried back to earth as the angelic chorus burst into song. Gwen flew higher and higher. The sunshine was blinding, birds were singing, and trees swayed in a gentle breeze. Gwen had never experienced such a beautiful day and her heart soared high as her wings lifted her aloft on a current of land-warmed air.

She couldn't wait to return to earth, and decided she was going to set up an Angelship in the heart of the Las Vegas Strip. From that strategic position, she would be able to reach out and help the sad, despondent, tragic humans who seemed drawn to this arid spot in the middle of the Mojave Desert. Gwen accepted her newly embraced mission with dignity-- and, yes, with total love. She now looked forward to helping the downtrodden gain a new sense of self-respect and a terrific new lease on life.

As she circled the gaudy city with all its lights, and came lower into the atmosphere, Gwen decided to set up shop in the pyramid with the beam of light shining high into the stratosphere. "Yes indeed", she said as she folded her wings beneath her sweater and entered the casino under the belly of the Sphinx. "Yes, indeed, there is a lot of need for my services here."

Just then, a frantic bellman yelled across the lobby at the bar manager headed to the casino bar. "Mac, watch where you're going! Can't you see the load I've got here?" The bar manager threw a look at the bellman that might have killed a more faint-hearted soul. What the heck was the bellman thinking? Insubordination was cause for immediate termination and he was a manager!

Gwen just smiled as she slipped behind the front desk in her new uniform. Yes, indeed, the pyramid was a cesspool of negative human emotion, and it was just the place she needed to be.